*For Rosie
who lent me her babies,
Lucy and Nicola.
M.W.*

*For Ruth
and Rowan,
my real inspiration
P.D.*

This edition is published and distributed exclusively
by Discovery Toys, Inc., Martinez, CA.
Published in Great Britain in 1990 by Walker Books Ltd., London
Text © 1990 Martin Waddell
Illustrations © 1990 Penny Dale
Printed in Hong Kong
ISBN 0939979-46-2

Rosie's Babies

Written by
Martin Waddell

Illustrated by
Penny Dale

DISCOVERY TOYS, INC.

Mom was putting the baby
to bed and Rosie said,
"I've got two babies and
you've only got one."
"Two, including you," said Mom.
"I'm not a baby, I'm four years old,"
said Rosie.
"Tell me about your babies,"
Mom said.

And Rosie said,
"My babies live in a bird's nest
and they are nearly as big as me.
They go out in the garden all by
themselves and sometimes they
make me angry!"
"Do they?" asked Mom.
"Yes, when they do silly things!"
said Rosie.
"What silly things do they do?"
asked Mom.

And Rosie said,
"My babies climbed a big mountain. That was silly, because they couldn't get down. They jumped and they bumped on their bottoms!"
"Silly babies," said Mom.
"Did they hurt themselves?"

And Rosie said,

"One of my babies hurt her knee.
I bandaged it up and she cried
and I said 'Never mind'
because I am nice."

"I'm sure you are," said Mom.

"What else do your babies do?"

And Rosie said,
"My babies drive cars that
are real ones and trucks and
boats. My babies are very
good drivers."
"What do your babies like
doing best?" asked Mom.

And Rosie said,
"My babies like swings and
rockers and dinosaurs. They go
to the park when it's dark and
there are no moms and dads
who can see, only me!"
"Gracious!" said Mom.
"Aren't they scared?"

And Rosie said,
"My babies are scared of the
big dogs, but I'm not. I go
GRRRRRRRRRRRRR!
and frighten the big dogs away."
"They are not very scared then?"
asked Mom.
"My babies know I will look
after them," said Rosie.
"I'm their mom."
"How do you look after them?"
Mom asked.

And Rosie said,
"I give them parties and I tell them
stories and I take them for walks
and I talk to them and I tell them
that I love them."
"That's a good way to look after
babies!" said Mom. "Do you make
them nice things to eat, like pies?"

And Rosie said,
"My babies make their own pies.
But they never eat them."
"What do they eat?" asked Mom.

And Rosie said,
"My babies eat apples and apples
and apples all the time. And
grapes and pears but they
don't like the seeds."
"Most babies don't," said Mom.
"Are you going to tell me
more about your babies?"

And Rosie thought and thought and thought and then Rosie said, "My babies have gone to bed."

"Just like this one," said Mom.

"I don't want to talk about my babies any more because they are asleep," said Rosie. "I don't want them to wake up or they'll cry."

"We could talk very softly," said Mom.

"Yes," said Rosie.

"What will we talk about?" asked Mom.

And Rosie said,

"ME!"